Happy 2nd
Birthday!
Calvin - we loved travelling to the
Badlands and Omaha zoo with
you last year. Can't
wait to see what
the next year
has in store!

Today's your birthday,
shout **HOORAY!**
It's your special day today!

Shout it **high** and shout it **low**.

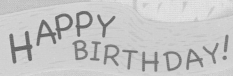

Shout to **everyone** you know!

HAPPY BIRTHDAY

Let's have a party, with a great big cake.
It's time for fun, make no mistake!

We love the things that make you, YOU!
We'll celebrate the whole day through!

Let's laugh and sing and have some fun.
It's a **happy day** for everyone!

Let's **dance** around and clap our hands,
and move in step to a marching band!

With every gift and treat and toy,
we'll **share** our love and hope and joy.

to:
from:

You are **special**, sweet, and kind,

with a gentle heart and a brilliant mind.

You fill our hearts with love and light.
We think of you both day...

and **night!**

From the **plants** that grow

to the **stars** in space,

there's nothing better
than your smiling face!

We love you more than **butterflies** and **bees**,

or the **fishies** in the ocean
and the **monkeys** in the trees!

We love you more than the
flowers of spring,

and the leaves of fall, and
EVERYTHING!

Today and **forever** . . .

Published by Sourcebooks Jabberwocky, an imprint of Sourcebooks, Inc.
P.O. Box 4410, Naperville, Illinois 60567-4410
(630) 961-3900
Fax: (630) 961-2168
jabberwockykids.com
sourcebooks.com

Source of Production: Heshan City, Guangdong Province, China
Date of Production: January 2018
Run Number: 5011553

Printed and bound in China.
LEO 10 9 8 7